W9-BEC-574

3650 Summit Boulevard
West Palm Beach, FL   33406-4198

530L

Dear Parents:

Congratulations! Your child is taking the first steps on an exciting journey. The destination? Independent reading!

STEP INTO READING® will help your child get there. The program offers five steps to reading success. Each step includes fun stories and colorful art or photographs. In addition to original fiction and books with favorite characters, there are Step into Reading Non-Fiction Readers, Phonics Readers and Boxed Sets, Sticker Readers, and Comic Readers—a complete literacy program with something to interest every child.

Learning to Read, Step by Step!

Ready to Read   Preschool–Kindergarten
• big type and easy words • rhyme and rhythm • picture clues
For children who know the alphabet and are eager to begin reading.

Reading with Help   Preschool–Grade 1
• basic vocabulary • short sentences • simple stories
For children who recognize familiar words and sound out new words with help.

Reading on Your Own   Grades 1–3
• engaging characters • easy-to-follow plots • popular topics
For children who are ready to read on their own.

Reading Paragraphs   Grades 2–3
• challenging vocabulary • short paragraphs • exciting stories
For newly independent readers who read simple sentences with confidence.

Ready for Chapters   Grades 2–4
• chapters • longer paragraphs • full-color art
For children who want to take the plunge into chapter books but still like colorful pictures.

STEP INTO READING® is designed to give every child a successful reading experience. The grade levels are only guides; children will progress through the steps at their own speed, developing confidence in their reading. The F&P Text Level on the back cover serves as another tool to help you choose the right book for your child.

Remember, a lifetime love of reading starts with a single step!

For Essie

Step into Reading, Random House, and the Random House colophon are registered trademarks of
Penguin Random House LLC.

Visit us on the Web!
StepIntoReading.com
rhcbooks.com

Educators and librarians, for a variety of teaching tools, visit us at
RHTeachersLibrarians.com

Library of Congress Cataloging-in-Publication Data
Buller, Jon, 1943– .
20,000 baseball cards under the sea / by Jon Buller and Susan Schade.
  p. cm. — (Step into reading. A step 4 book)
Summary: Roger's friend Kenneth uses an unusual sea vehicle of his own design to take them to
an underwater cave, where a cache of old loot gathered by the mermaids turns out to contain a lot
of very valuable old baseball cards.
ISBN 978-0-679-81569-3 (trade) — ISBN 978-0-679-91569-0 (lib. bdg.)
[1. Inventors—Fiction. 2. Buried treasure—Fiction. 3. Baseball cards—Fiction.]
I. Title: Twenty thousand baseball cards under the sea. II. Schade, Susan. III. Title.
IV. Series: Step into reading. Step 4 book.
PZ7.B9135 Aaf 2003 [E]—dc21 2002015227

MANUFACTURED IN CHINA 38 37 36 35 34 33 32

This book has been officially leveled by using the F&P Text Level Gradient™ Leveling System.

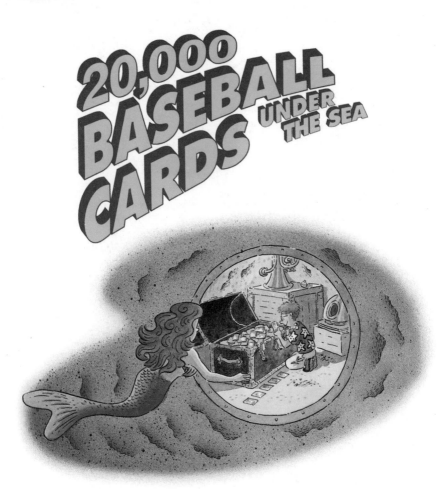

20,000 BASEBALL CARDS UNDER THE SEA

by Jon Buller
and Susan Schade

Random House 🏠 New York

I'm a collector.

I collect baseball cards, dinosaurs,
comic books, robots, and cars.

My friend Kenneth is a collector too.

One day I was going to visit Kenneth after school.

I was dreaming about what I could buy if I won the lottery. Would I buy a Corvette, a Rolls-Royce, or a Jeep?

I wasn't looking where I was going.

Yikes! I almost stepped on a big black snake! At least it looked like a snake. But it was nothing but an old strip of rubber.

I decided to give it to Kenneth. He would find a use for it.

What Kenneth collects is junk. He likes to make stuff out of it.
Kenneth is into recycling.

He was really happy when I brought him the strip of rubber.

"I can use that," he said, and he hung it over a hook.

We went into the kitchen.

Kenneth always makes me fish cakes with maple syrup. He knows how much I like them. He likes them too.

"So, Roger, how was school today?" he asked me.

I always tell him about my troubles in school. "I was the last kid picked for basketball," I said. "Even after the girls. And the lunch was ravioli."

Then Kenneth tells me about his troubles.

"Do you know they raised my taxes to $2,000? Where am I going to get $2,000? This country is in bad shape. In fact, this whole planet is a mess."

After we ate we went outside. Kenneth
brought the strip of rubber and we went
to look at his latest project.

It looked like a giant pill on wheels. Kenneth started gluing the rubber around the front end. "This strip is just what I needed for the door," he said.

When he was done he opened the
door and climbed in. "Come on, Roger,"
he said, "let's try her out!"

I had never tried any of Kenneth's
contraptions before.

I wasn't sure I wanted to. But I
crawled inside anyway.

Kenneth turned a key. The whole contraption rattled and shook. We started moving out of Kenneth's backyard and onto the beach.

Uh-oh! We were headed right for
the water.

We went into the water.

We went UNDER the water!

I was under the sea in a homemade submarine.

A little stream of brownish water bubbled through a crack in the wall.

"Uh, Kenneth." I touched his sleeve and pointed to the leak.

"No problem," he said, handing me a jar. "Slap some of this gunk on there, will you?"

I slapped some of the gunk on it, and the leak stopped.

Then I looked out the window. It was
beautiful! We were cruising above the
ocean floor. The scenery was awesome.

Light rays rippled through the water. Plants swayed back and forth. A mermaid swam past the window. A MERMAID?

"Hey!" I cried. "That was a…"

"I know," Kenneth said. "Lots of them down here."

I kept looking. He was right.

After a while we ran right into a rocky wall and stopped.

"Uh-oh!" I said.

"Uh-oh, nothing," said Kenneth. "This is where we get out."

He opened the door.

"Hey!" I cried. I expected a big flood, but nothing happened. The rubber strip made a tight seal against the wall.

We were looking at another door. It was fitted into the rock wall.

Kenneth opened it, and we crawled into an underwater cavern.

It was full of junk! "How do you like my storage shed?" Kenneth asked me.

I was speechless.

"Where does all this stuff come from?"
I finally asked. "How did it get here?"

"It comes from old shipwrecks. The
merpeople collect it for me. And I make
things for them. We have a nice
arrangement."

I looked out the window. Some of the
merpeople were driving by in funny
contraptions. I recognized Kenneth's work.

"Have a look around, Roger," he said.
"Let me know if you see anything you
want."

OH BOY!

There was a lot of neat stuff. Hats and
boots and fishhooks. And towels and
books and big ropes and diving gear.
And propellers and broken chairs and
a tuba.

There were ships' instruments made
of polished wood with gears and dials.
I wasn't sure what they were for, but
I liked them a lot.

In one corner there were some old books and magazines piled up on a big wooden trunk. They were all dusty.

I moved the books and magazines and opened the trunk.

It was full of unopened packs of baseball cards! I had found something I wanted all right.

I opened one of the packs.

The bubble gum was pretty stale.
But the top card was the 1951 Tony Pudnik
rookie card!

Can you believe it?

In my baseball-card catalog there's
a whole page on that card. It's worth
$5,000! No kidding.

I almost swallowed my gum.

I was counting out the packs and scratching numbers in the sand when Kenneth called me.

"Hey, Roger!"

"Just give me five more minutes!" I shouted.

"Five minutes?" said Kenneth. "You can have fifty years! We're staying!"

"Staying? You mean underwater? FOREVER?"

"Why not?" said Kenneth. "Think about it. No more taxes! No more worries. Mermaids. Plenty of junk. No more school."

No school. That did make me think. Except…

"Are there other kids down here?" I asked.

"Sure," said Kenneth. "Merkids!"

He waved his hand toward the porthole. A mermaid girl was swimming by.

She saw me. She called her friend over. They were both looking at me and pointing and laughing.

I danced the hokey-pokey for them.
They loved it.

I was thinking maybe it would be okay to live underwater for a while. Of course I would have to call my mother.

Then I remembered the baseball cards.

"Oh heck," I said. "I was going to sell some of these cards and buy a Corvette."

Kenneth laughed and laughed.

"No, really," I said. "Don't you know
what these are worth? Tony Pudnik is
going for $5,000! And you could probably
get $1,500 for this one, maybe $2,000.
You've got about 20,000 cards here, and
even if they sold for only $10 apiece,
that would be $200,000!"

Kenneth looked sort of excited.

"You've got a lot of valuable stuff down
here," I said. "These old comics are worth
a lot too."

"So I could pay my taxes," he said slowly.

"No problem," I said.

"I could keep my house and still visit the merpeople," said Kenneth. "Okay, we'll go fifty-fifty."

I thought that was pretty generous. We shook hands on it.

So that's how I got my Corvette.

Of course I don't have my license yet. But sometimes I let my mother drive me around.

And I still have the Tony Pudnik rookie card, too.

Some things are worth more than money.